MW00934584

Copyright © 2014 Disney Enterprises, Inc. All rights reserved.
Published by Disney Press, an imprint of Disney Book Group. No part of this book may
be reproduced or transmitted in any form or by any means, electronic or mechanical,
including photocopying, recording, or by any information storage and retrieval system,
without written permission from the publisher. For information address
Disney Press, 1101 Flower Street, Glendale, California 91201.

First Edition 10 9 8 7 6 5 4 3 2 1

ISBN 978-1-4231-8400-3
F322-8368-0-14087

Printed in the USA
For more Disney Press fun,
visit www.disneybooks.com

Disney
MINNIE IN PARIS

Written by
SHEILA SWEENY HIGGINSON

Illustrated by
MIKE WALL

Disney PRESS
New York • Los Angeles

It's Fashion Week in PARIS!

All the top designers are busy preparing for their shows.

And Minnie has been invited to go, too!

THE HOUSE OF
CUCKOO CHANEL

Mademoiselle Minerva Mouse

You have been
invited to show your bows
at our Fashion Week event
in Paris, France.

"**Ooh la la!**" says Cuckoo-Loca.

"Your bows will be the hit of the runway!" Daisy cheers.

"**Paris!** Oh, my," Minnie sighs. "Every bow will need to have style.
Every bow will need to have flair."

Minnie designs a new series of fashionable bows.

Daisy and Cuckoo-Loca snip...

and staple...

and sew.

Everything is ready—just in the nick of time.

Millie and Melody grab the biggest suitcase they can find.

Minnie and her crew race to the airport.

Look who else is going to Paris . . .

Penguini the Magnificent!

LONDON FLIGHT DELAYED

★ PARIS FLIGHT 010 BOARDING NOW!!

◀GATE 813

"Have a **magical** day!" Minnie calls to him as she chases after Millie and Melody.

Finally, it's time to take off!

The plane soars over the ocean . . .

and lands in France.

Daisy grabs the suitcase.

Cuckoo-Loca hails a taxi.

Minnie checks in to the hotel,

and Millie and Melody find the room.

Uh-oh!

Daisy must have picked up Penguini's suitcase by mistake.

Now Minnie has no bows for the fashion show!

This is a
BOW-TASTROPHE!

One by one, Penguini's bunnies hop out of the suitcase.

"Don't open that door!" Minnie says to her nieces.

But it's too late. The bunnies are gone!

"We'll round up the bunnies," Minnie says.

"Daisy, you and Cuckoo-Loca find some ribbon.

We need to make new bows."

Millie and Melody chase one bunny

down a busy street.

"Look, girls! It's the

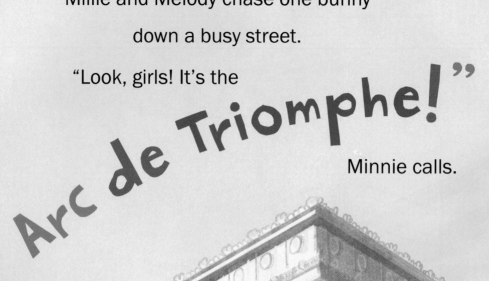

Minnie calls.

Millie and Melody follow two bunnies onto a riverboat.

"The Seine River!" sighs Minnie.

"NOTRE DAME CATHEDRAL!"

Minnie gasps. *"C'est magnifique!"*

Three bunnies scamper through a crowd of tourists.

Millie, Melody, and Minnie chase after them.

"Should we go help them, Daisy?" Cuckoo-Loca asks.

"It looks like Minnie and the girls are doing fine," Daisy says.

"There's one more shop we need to visit, anyway."

The girls find four bunnies in a field of flowers at the

Jardin des Tuileries.

"Oh, my," says Minnie. "These colors are like the

beautiful paintings inside the museum."

Melody and Millie head inside the museum and run down the hall after five bunnies.

"THE LOUVRE!

THE MINNIE LISA

I've always wanted to see the *Minnie Lisa*," says Minnie as she gets a quick look at the famous painting.

Six bunnies crash into a cart of croissants.

"Bon appétit!"

Minnie calls, taking one last bite of her omelet.

Seven bunnies pile onto a puppet-filled stage.

"What merry marionettes!"

Minnie applauds. "Now get those bunnies, girls!"

Minnie and her nieces tiptoe after eight
bunnies on a tightrope at the
Cirque de Paris.

"Jugglers and acrobats and clowns—
oh, my!" Minnie cries.

Millie sees nine bunnies at the Metro.

"Next stop, Champs-de-Mars!" Minnie says.

THE EIFFEL TOWER

"We've got the last ten bunnies," Minnie says.

"Now it's time to head back to the hotel!"

Minnie has a lot of bows to make and
not a lot of time to make them!

Millie and Daisy **snip.**

Melody and Cuckoo-Loca **staple.**

Minnie **sews.**

Everything's ready—just in the nick of time.

It's off to the show!

They hop into a taxi.

Penguini the Magnificent is right behind them.

He's been looking all over Paris for his bunnies—

and he's finally spotted them!

At the show,
Daisy gathers the models.

Minnie ties on the bows.

Cuckoo-Loca crosses her wings for good luck.

Minnie's new bows are perfectly Parisian—made from souvenirs she gathered on the great bunny chase.